Learning to Read, Step by Step!

Ready to Read Preschool–Kindergarten
• big type and easy words • rhyme and rhythm • picture clues
For children who know the alphabet and are eager to begin reading.

Reading with Help Preschool–Grade 1
• basic vocabulary • short sentences • simple stories
For children who recognize familiar words and sound out new words with help.

Reading on Your Own Grades 1–3
• engaging characters • easy-to-follow plots • popular topics
For children who are ready to read on their own.

Reading Paragraphs Grades 2–3
• challenging vocabulary • short paragraphs • exciting stories
For newly independent readers who read simple sentences with confidence.

Ready for Chapters Grades 2–4
• chapters • longer paragraphs • full-color art
For children who want to take the plunge into chapter books but still like colorful pictures.

STEP INTO READING® is designed to give every child a successful reading experience. The grade levels are only guides; children will progress through the steps at their own speed, developing confidence in their reading. The F&P Text Level on the back cover serves as another tool to help you choose the right book for your child.

Remember, a lifetime love of reading starts with a single step!

For Aunt Christine—D.M.

To my children, Sidesel Emilie, Gabriel,
and Rumle Michael—M.E.

Text copyright © 2020 by Diana Murray
Cover art and interior illustrations copyright © 2020 by Mette Engell

All rights reserved. Published in the United States by Random House Children's Books, a division of Penguin Random House LLC, New York.

Step into Reading, Random House, and the Random House colophon are registered trademarks of Penguin Random House LLC.

Visit us on the Web!
StepIntoReading.com
rhcbooks.com

Educators and librarians, for a variety of teaching tools, visit us at RHTeachersLibrarians.com

Library of Congress Cataloging-in-Publication Data
Names: Murray, Diana, author. | Engell, Mette, illustrator.
Title: Double the dinosaurs / by Diana Murray ; illustrated by Mette Engell.
Description: New York : Random House, [2020] | Series: Step into reading. Step 1 | Audience: Ages 4–6. | Audience: Grades K–1. | Summary: In this story that introduces the fundamentals of addition and the concept of doubling, a swamp becomes quite crowded as the number of dinosaurs doubles each time, from one to sixty-four.
Identifiers: LCCN 2019041351 | ISBN 978-0-525-64870-3 (trade paperback) | ISBN 978-0-525-64871-0 (library binding) | ISBN 978-0-525-64872-7 (ebook)
Subjects: CYAC: Stories in rhyme. | Addition—Fiction. | Multiplication—Fiction. | Dinosaurs—Fiction.
Classification: LCC PZ8.3.M9362 Dp 2020 | DDC [E]—dc23

Printed in the United States of America
10 9 8 7 6 5 4 3 2

This book has been officially leveled by using the F&P Text Level Gradient™ Leveling System.

Double the Dinosaurs

by Diana Murray

illustrated by Mette Engell

Random House 🏠 New York

Hot, sunny day.

Cool, muddy shore.

All is quiet.

Then suddenly . . .

ROAR!

One jumbo dinosaur

heads for the swamp.

Double the dinosaur. . . .

Double the STOMP!

Two romping dinosaurs
leap through the mud.

Double the dinosaurs. . . .

Double the THUD!

Four roaring dinosaurs
skip, hop, and tumble.

Double the dinosaurs. . . .

Double the RUMBLE!

Eight playful dinosaurs,
quick as a flash!

Double the dinosaurs. . . .

Double the SPLASH!

Sixteen loud dinosaurs
munch on some lunch.

Double the dinosaurs. . . .

Double the CRUNCH!

Thirty-two dinosaurs yawning and roaring.

Double the dinosaurs. . . .

Double the SNORING!

Sixty-four dinosaurs,
cozy as any.

Double the dinosaurs. . . .

Stop! Way too many!
The swamp is too
crowded.
This is no fun!

Away they
all run . . .

. . . and then
there are none.